MY DAD'S JOB

STORY BY **Peter Glassman**   PICTURES BY **Timothy Bush**

Simon & Schuster Books for Young Readers

NEW YORK   LONDON   TORONTO   SYDNEY   SINGAPORE   Simon & NEW YORK

I wish I could go to work with my dad.
He's always talking about his job,
and it sounds like he has fun every day.

On Monday, when Dad came home from work,

he told Mom that he had been put on a great team.

After dinner I asked my
brother what games
Dad's team played.

My brother said Dad's team didn't play games,

but I'm not so sure—even if he *is* older than me.

On Tuesday, Dad came home from work late.

He said his company
was fighting off a
hostile takeover.

While my sister and I were taking out the garbage,
I asked her if Dad would let me help fight off the
raiders who were trying to take over his company.

She said that they weren't those kind of raiders.
But I'm not so sure—even if she *is* stronger than me.

On Wednesday, Dad was really tired.
He told Mom that the market was up and down and
that the bulls and bears were giving everyone a wild ride.

As I was getting ready for bed,
I asked Mom if I could ride
some of Dad's bulls and bears.

Mom said they weren't those
type of bulls and bears.

But I'm not so sure
—even if she *is* my mom!

So on Thursday, when Dad started talking about
buying futures . . .

I decided to find out for myself.

"Dad, can I go to work with you tomorrow?"
I asked as he tucked me in.

"Of course," he said. "I can use your help."

All the way to work I wanted to ask him if his job was as much fun as it sounded, but I was scared.

What if I was wrong? I just wasn't sure. When we finally arrived at his office, I was less sure than ever.

It didn't look like the kind of place where you'd have a lot of fun.

It didn't look like the kind of place where you'd have *any* fun.

Then we went in . . .

PULL

I wish I could go to work with my dad every day.

Maybe someday I will.

team: a group of people who work together to achieve a common goal

company: a group of people who work together to create a product (like baseballs, ice cream, or movies) or to perform a service (like painting a house, taking people on trips by airplane, or teaching a class)

hostile takeover: a forceful attempt by one company to take control of another company

raiders: those who attempt a hostile takeover

market: a place where people come together to sell things; in business there are stock markets (where shares in the ownership of a company are sold) and commodity markets (where companies and individuals buy and sell large amounts of such products as orange juice, coffee, and heating oil), as well as **futures** markets (where people make a promise to buy a product like orange juice, coffee, or heating oil at a specific price in the future)

bull market: a market in which prices are going up (meaning the stocks or products being sold are getting more expensive)

bear market: a market in which prices are going down (meaning the stocks or products being sold are getting less expensive)

For my dad, Robert Martin Glassman, who took me to work and taught me that when you like your work, it's called fun. —P. G.

For my dad, still with us in spirit—T. B.

SIMON & SCHUSTER BOOKS FOR YOUNG READERS
An imprint of Simon & Schuster Children's Publishing Division
1230 Avenue of the Americas, New York, New York 10020
Text copyright © 2003 by Peter Glassman
Illustrations copyright © 2003 by Timothy Bush
SIMON & SCHUSTER BOOKS FOR YOUNG READERS is a trademark of Simon & Schuster.
Book design by Greg Stadnyk
The text of this book is set in Weidemann.
The illustrations are rendered in watercolor.
Manufactured in China
2 4 6 8 10 9 7 5 3 1
Library of Congress Cataloging-in-Publication Data
My dad's job / by Peter Glassman ; illustrated by Timothy Bush.
p. cm.
Summary: Listening to his father talk about his job, a young boy imagines all the fun he must have at work every day.
ISBN 0-689-82890-X
[1. Work—Fiction. 2. Fathers—Fiction.] I. Bush, Timothy, ill. II Title.
PZ7.G481447 Dad 2002
[E]—dc21   2001020132